MATTHEW AND THE MIDNIGHT TOW TRUCK

MATTHEW AND THE

Midnight Tow Truck

Story
Allen Morgan

Art
Michael Martchenko

ANNICK PRESS LTD.
Toronto • New York • Vancouver

Twelfth printing, May 1999

Annick Press Ltd.

We acknowledge the support of the Canada Council for the Arts for our publishing program. We also thank the Ontario Arts Council.

Cataloguing in Publication Data
Morgan, Allen, 1946-
Matthew and the midnight tow truck

(Matthew's midnight adventure series)
ISBN 0-920303-00-5 (bound) ISBN 0-920303-01-3 (pbk.)

I. Martchenko, Michael. II. Title. III. Series:
Morgan, Allen, 1946- Matthew's midnight
adventure series.

PS8576.073M38 1984 jC813'.54 C84-098921-0
PZ7.M67Ma 1984

Distributed in Canada by:
Firefly Books Ltd.
3680 Victoria Park Avenue
Willowdale, ON
M2H 3K1

Published in the U.S.A. by Annick Press (U.S.) Ltd.
Distributed in the U.S.A. by:
Firefly Books (U.S.) Inc.
P.O. Box 1338
Ellicott Station
Buffalo, NY 14205

Printed and bound in Canada by
Friesens, Altona, Manitoba.

For Matthew M.

One night, Matthew was playing with his cars in the kitchen while he waited for his supper to cook. First he took his tow truck and hooked onto a station wagon. He towed it right up onto the table top and dropped it off on his plate. Then he drove back down to get another one. Towing all his cars away made Matthew feel hungry, so he told his mother that they needed something special for dessert.

“Let’s go down to the store and get some red licorice,” he said.

“Sorry,” said his mother. “You’ve had enough candy already today. You don’t need any more.”

Matthew didn’t agree at all. He told his mother that he needed red licorice a lot, but she just shook her head.

“Not tonight,” she said. “Tonight you’re having fruit cocktail. Now take those cars off your plate so I can serve supper.”

Later that night just before bedtime, when Matthew was counting his cars, he discovered that one of his vans was missing. He told his mother right away and they looked all around the bedroom for it. But even though they looked everywhere, they couldn't find Matthew's missing van.

"It's getting late," said his mother finally. "I'm afraid it's time to go to bed. We'll have to find your van some other time."

"But it's my very best one," Matthew told his mother, as she tucked him in. "I'll bet it's lost for good now, I'll bet I never see it again."

His mother kissed him goodnight and told him not to worry.

"You can look for it when you wake up," she said, as she turned out the light. "It's bound to turn up one way or another."

Matthew hoped that she was right. Even so, when he fell asleep, he was feeling a little sad.

Later that night, just after midnight, Matthew woke up. He saw a flashing red light shining in through his window, so he jumped out of bed and went to see what was happening outside.

A big black midnight tow truck was standing in the middle of the street, right in front of Matthew's house. The driver was working on one of the cars that was parked at the curb. He was trying to hook onto the bumper, but the hook was too big and it kept slipping off.

The midnight tow-truck driver was just about to give up when he looked up and saw Matthew at the window. His face broke into a great big grin then.

"Hey, kid!" he shouted up at Matthew. "Come on outside here, will ya? I'm going to need some help hooking this one!"

Matthew went downstairs. He went very quietly because he didn't want to wake up his mother. He put on his boots and his jacket and then he went outside. The midnight tow-truck driver was waiting for him. He slapped Matthew on the back.

"Hi, kid!" he said. "Glad you could make it. This job is going to take the two of us. Grab the hook, will ya?"

Matthew grabbed the hook and held it on the bumper while the midnight tow-truck driver worked the crank. In no time at all the job was done and the car was ready to be towed away.

“Not bad, kid, not bad at all,” said the midnight tow-truck driver. “You do good work. Want to help me hook some more cars?”

“Sure!” said Matthew, and he climbed up into the front seat.

Matthew and the midnight tow-truck driver went all around the city that night, hooking cars together. First they got a station wagon. Then they picked up a van. Matthew was feeling a little hungry from all the work. So was the midnight tow-truck driver.

“Let’s pull over and have a snack,” he suggested.

They stopped at an empty parking lot just beside the railroad tracks. The midnight tow-truck driver got out his lunchbox and opened it. The lunchbox was full of red licorice.

"Take some," said the midnight tow-truck driver. "Take as much as you need. You can never get enough red licorice, you know. It's good for you and it gives you big muscles."

Matthew and the midnight tow-truck driver sat and ate red licorice for a while.

"What do you do with all the cars you hook?" asked Matthew.

"I collect them," said the midnight tow-truck driver. "I'm trying to get one of every kind, but I pick up doubles sometimes so I can trade with the other guys."

Just then, another tow truck drove into the lot and the man that was driving it called over to them.

"Hey, that's a nice-looking station wagon you got hooked there," he shouted. "What do you want for it?"

"You got any jeeps?" asked the midnight tow-truck driver.

"Sure I got jeeps," the man answered. "All kinds of them!"

"Well, come over to my place tomorrow after lunch," the midnight tow-truck driver told him. "We can trade."

"I'll be there," promised the other man, and then he drove away.

When the red licorice was all gone, the midnight tow-truck driver drove over to a car wash. Matthew helped him unhook the cars they were towing and then they pushed them inside.

The midnight tow-truck driver opened a secret door on the wall of the car wash and Matthew saw a special button there. “What’s that for?” he asked.

“That button makes the car wash shrink the cars,” said the midnight tow-truck driver, and he reached in and pushed it.

The car wash started to work. Water splashed and the big brushes began to spin. Special shrinking soap squirted out of some secret nozzles and covered the cars.

Sure enough, when the cars came out the other end they were all shrunk down to pocket size.

The midnight tow-truck driver picked them up and dried them off with his handkerchief. He grinned at Matthew.

"Listen, kid, I'll tell you what. You helped me hook three cars tonight. So I was wondering, why don't you just keep one for yourself? Take it home with you, what do you think?"

Matthew thought it was a good idea. He took the van and put it in his jacket pocket.

It was almost morning, so the midnight tow-truck driver drove Matthew home and dropped him off.

"I was thinking," said Matthew. "My mother has a car, it's that one over there. You wouldn't tow it away by mistake some night, would you?"

"Kid, I'd never!" said the midnight tow-truck driver.

"What about the other guys?" asked Matthew.

"Good thing you mentioned it," said the midnight tow-truck driver. "I'll tell them to lay off, too. Just stick a piece of red licorice under the windshield wiper so they'll know it's yours."

Matthew promised that he would, all right. He said goodnight, and then he went inside. He took off his boots, he hung up his jacket, and then he went upstairs and got into bed. Soon he was fast asleep.

Later that morning around about six, Matthew woke up again. He ran downstairs and checked his jacket. Sure enough, the van was there in his pocket, just the way he remembered it. So Matthew brought his van upstairs to show to his mother.

“Time to get up!” Matthew told her. “Look! I found my van!” “Your what?” asked his mother, and she sat up in bed. “Oh, your van, that’s nice,” she said, and she lay back in bed and tried to go back to sleep.

But Matthew didn't let her. "The van was in my jacket pocket!" he said. "I bet you'll never guess how it got there!"

Matthew was right. His mother couldn't guess, so Matthew had to tell her. She was very interested to hear the story.

"You certainly were busy last night," she said.

"We hooked a lot of cars, all right," agreed Matthew. "But you don't have to worry about your car. The midnight tow-truck driver is going to make sure that nobody gets it."

"Well, I'm glad to hear that," said his mother.

"The only thing is, we'll need some red licorice just to make sure," said Matthew, and he explained what they had to do.

“I guess we’ll have to go down to the store and buy some,” said his mother. “It looks like we really need some red licorice, after all.”

“Yes, we do,” said Matthew, and he gave his mother a great big hug.

Other books by Allen Morgan:

Matthew and the Midnight Turkeys
Matthew and the Midnight Money Van
Daddy-Care
Nicole's Boat
Andrew and the Wild Bikes